Selected Poems of
Seokwoo Whang – English Translation

Universe
Full of
Smile

Editor's Notes

•This anthology of Seokwoo Whang's Poetry: English Edition consists of important poems selected by the editors, from the late Seokwoo Whang's *Ode to Nature*(1929) and other poetic works written and published by him.

•The Korean texts are the earliest possible versions which are believed to be closer to the original works. Yet the spacing followed the current spelling system. (This is due to that many of the poet's works were in the earlier form of modern Korean language with its grammar that was quite different from the present shape of it.)

•The anthology contains about 70 poems translated, including 30 Korean originals sorted out from English translation poems.

Selected Poems of
Seokwoo Whang – English Translation

Universe
Full of
Smile

Compiled by **Edou Park**
Translated by **Shinkwon Cho**

Forest of Time

It was the summer of 2014 when I met Hyoyoung Whang, in Washington, D.C., the third son of Seokwoo Whang, 'Sangatab'(i.e. Ivory Tower), the very poet we are dealing with. He hinted that he had enjoyed the paternal love not that much from his childhood, due to the poet's Bohemian life style. Even worse, Hyoyoung's mother also had left for the daughter's home in the United States, he said, so he spent well over his adolescence, feeling like an orphan; and that would become his lifelong bitterness.

At any rate, Hyoyoung came to miss the late father's love badly during his own immigrant life for more than 40 years, pondering over the poet's life story and legacy to pass on to his descendants. At such a right time I could meet him and hand him over a short essay I wrote about Seokwoo's poetical works [which was published by Literary House, Seoul], then had a long talk regarding the poet. That's how we have come now to bring out Seokwoo Whang's poetry anthology in an English translation.

Seokwoo Whang(1895-1959) was in his full scale activity around 1920, based on *Pehhuh*(i.e. Ruins), a literary coterie magazine. Frequenting Seoul and Tokyo, impassioned by neo-culture and neo-literature from the West, while anguished with ideology under Japan's colonial rule, he absorbed in criticism and writing free verses. He left whole lot of works besides the ones contained in *Ode to Nature* (1929). After the 1945 Liberation, he also actively involved in politics and education, yet still continued to write.

Whang's poetry, along with his *Pehhuh* junto, centuralized in cultivating free verses, on the level of passing from the western literature, especially from Decadence. Yet his poetic conception and cosmical imagination caused his own idiosyncratic beauty. Notably in many works from *Ode to Nature*, he developed a unique sphere with his cosmic imagery and thinking process, dealing with objects in Nature or human characters.

Since Seokwoo Whang had died of his chronic disease in 1959, the literary estimation on his poetry was lowered down more relatively than his contemporary coterie poets Kim Uhg, Oh Sangsoon, and Kim Youngnang were.

Most recently in the world of Korean literature, revaluation on Whang's historical legacy and the works develops lively ever. Study on Seokwoo Whang, Wootaeg Jeong's thesis and many treatises and essays have been published.

Edou Park, The Compiler & Poet

• Seokwoo Whang

1895 : Born to Whang 16 Cheonyeon Dong, Gyeongsungbu (Seoul under Japanese colonial period)

1911 : Enters Boseong Vocational School, studies for 3 years, but gets expelled after the school's cap-badge incident occurred by Japanese oppression.

1914-1915 : Visit to Japan

1916 : January 16. Issues bimonthly *Geundaesajo*(Trend of Recent Thoughts)

1918 : Takes part in *Miraesa* led by Miki Rohu(三木露風, 1889-1964), a Japanese symbolical poet.

1919 : February. Launches *Samkwang*(Three Lights), a bulletin of Ragwoohoeh(i.e. Happy Friendship), a Korean foreign students' fellowship in Tokyo, together with Hong Young-woo, Yoo Jiyoung, Lee Byeongdo.

1920 : April. Enters Waseda University(Vocational Dept.):

majoring in politico-economics

1921 :

May. Launches *Jangmichon*(Rose Village) (Coterie: Byeon Youngro, Noh Jayoung, Park Jonghwa, Park younghee, Jeong Taesin, Lee Hoon, Oh Sangsoon)

November 25. Gets arrested together with Won Jongrin, Jo Yonghee, Jeong Jaedal, while distributing propaganda leaflets on culturalism movement.

1922 :

July. Founds *Pehhuh*, the literary coterie mag(together with Kim Uhg, Namgung Byeok, Oh Sangsoon, Lee Byeongdo).

September. Dropped from the school. Active in writing for several media: "Painful Stay" for March issue of *Samkwang*, "Come, Lover to Snow?", "A Musical Sketch" for the sixth issue of *Changjo*.

1927 :

February. In Changchun, Manchuria, takes office as vice

president of Korean-Manchurian Immigrant Farmers Protection Institute.

October. Launches *Joseon Sidan*(World of Korean Poems).

1945 : Takes the post of Editor-in-Chief of *Daedong Newspaper*.

December. Takes part in General Affairs Department of National Foundation Fund.

1946 : March. Joins in Pan-Korean Literary Fellowship.

1953 : April. Becomes the Dean of Kukmin University.

1955-1958 : Dedicated to write for *Dong-A Ilbo*(i.e. East Asia Daily News), *Hyundai Munhak* (i.e. Modern Literature), etc.

1959 : April. Passes away due to a chronic disease.

Edou Park, The Compiler & Poet

Contents

 The Sun Sets

PART II   Flowers by the Mountain Road at Nightfall

PART III

Symphony for Flowers

On the Poet Seokwoo Whang

**PART
I**

The Sun Sets

Fallen Leaves

Fallen leaves are

Postpartum cleansing

Done

By grass and trees.

Fallen leaves are

The biographies by grass and trees

Of their happy life of labor,

Written on the ground in bold letters.

Fog

Fog is

Blindfolding all creatures

On the earth

With grey mesh,

While the sky is undressed to change.

★ 한글본 시 126쪽

Respect Winter

Respect winter.

Winter is a great farmer—

A farmer to plant spring:

Its comely life in the frozen ground!

Then snow is his detoxified fertilizer,

And the midwinter wind the vigorous cow moo, plowing a field!

★ 한글본 시 127쪽

Fireflies

Fireflies are flying around so well.

They are flashing low in the air,

Twinkling,

Turning on and off their lights

On the field,

By the stream,

And between the twigs.

They are like stunt planes in the night.

So quite and well they fly!

Oh, who are riding

On their wings—

From whence and whither?

★ 한글본 시 128쪽

Cat with Blue Hair

One day, from under the shade of desert grove,

The napping spot for my soul,

A cat with blue hair

Peered into my lonesome heart,

Saying:

(Hey, child, all your

Agony and all your fate

I will parboil them in my love,

Love boiling

Like a hot spring,

Only if your heart

Becomes the sun

Of our world,

Only if it becomes Christ.)

★ 한글본 시 129쪽

The Carrier Couple

Day is husband, Night is his wife!

—a couple in everlasting separation.

Do they same delivery service, though:

Day delivers vigor and vitality,

While Night brings peaceful sleep.

They divided the earth into two sides,

Day working in the country of the sun;

Night, in the country of the stars and the moon.

★ 한글본 시 130쪽

The Sun Sets

Like the night shadows on the window

Of twittering young newly-weds' room dim out, the sun sets,

The sun sets.

Hey, lover, laugh through the night.

I'll spread my pure heart that's like an innocent virgin's

flesh

And show you to dazzle your eyes.

Yet now, in my heart,

Remains only a trace of the kiss just I've got,

Dispirited, weakened and deplored

At sunset.

Hey, lover, laugh through the night.

With my soft, spreaded heart

I will cover your pestered lonesome soul

Like covering the sweet autumn evening moon.

Hey, lover, laugh through the night.

On the foundation of your laughter, I would build a small tent
To talk in and sleep sweet-as-honey in,
Until the mere dot of the dawn, far from the end of the earth,
Reappears before our souls.

Hey, lover, laugh through the night.
That smile of yours is like the disarming wind in the spring evening
Which would make the hair of girl,
Who rests her chin in her hand,
Enraptured with first love, dance,
And that smile of yours
Is like the rainbow embroidered on my heart after tears cleared away.

Hey, lover, laugh through the night.

With the pen of updated golden wisdom,

Dipped into the ink of your crystal clear smile,

I will draw your face,

On my mind whiter than snow,

Your lengthy lifetime,

Beginning with the preface of the kiss at dusk

In pure red, or deep blue, or sky blue,

In your most favorite color.

Well, in that trace of the deplored kiss.

Hey, lover, laugh through the night.

Till my mind gets intoxicated and falls

I would pluck the strings of your laugh to play that have

the latent energy

Like the scents of roses; like the fragrance of a virgin's flesh.

Laugh, Lover; the sun sets.

Hey, lover, laugh through the night.

Since your laughter would be a veil of heat shimmer to cover my heart,

Would it be a floral blind hung at the door of my mind,

I'd wear pretty make-up behind it.

Since your laughter might be a storm or cloud moving toward some countries,

I would put nimbly on it my soul.

As your laughter is a certain agent to heal my inner wounds

I would plunge into the boiling pot of it.

Would your smile be a clue to a world, the commentary of a song on its life,

More than anything, will I be all ears for it.

Should your smile be the secret album of your sorrows

Open solely to me,

I will weep till my whole heart be immersed in the flood of tears.

Laugh, Lover, the sun sets.

Universe full of Smile

One early summer morning, I'd wake up and open my eyes,

So would the little cat at bedside and meow.

As I lift up my head, open the window and look down
upon the yard,

Moss roses near the wall with their petals open seem to
giggle and chatter cutely.

The sky would also open its opaque eyelids smilingly,

Then from under the distant hill would rise the morning
sun, too,

With its beaming face.

It's the moment when the whole world wakes and beams up;

The universe is full of smile.

★ 한글본 시 131쪽

Blossoms of Snow

Snowflakes are

The butterflies from the country of clouds,

Flying in winter.

But they felt sad

There were no flowers on the earth,

Thus clustering around grasses, twigs and branches

To become snow flowers themselves.

The Dawn

It is not that the sun rises in the dawn.

Rather, is the dawn when the sunshines bloom like a morning glory.

The dawn is to unfold the screen of ten thousand picture panels of sunlight.

The dawn is when the sun breathes out fragrance of orange.

The dawn is the light to all lives shone still far from sunbeams.

And is the dawn the color in the universe's cheeks, intoxicated by the first scent of the sun.

★ 한글본 시 136쪽

The Solar System and the Earth

Our solar system

In the universe

Is the Geumkang Mountains of starry world.

Earth as in the solar system

Is the miniature paradise of the universe; small utopia,

With its flowers in full bloom.

The Miniature Universe and
the Great Universe

The universe visible to ordinary sight is

Only the celestial bodies around the solar system.

That is called the 'island universe.' •

In this miniature universe are the stellar system of the
constellation Hercules

And two hundred million stars,

Stately sitting around high above like folding screens;

Below them are our moon, the sun and the earth,

Cutely floating around like tiny balloons.

And out of this cosmos is the great universe

Where galaxies are infinitely spreaded hither and thither;

Among them all island universes contain myriads of nebulae,

Dispersed by small stars as the grains of sand in the Ganges,

Suns,

And the world of creatures;

Their kinds and the numbers are dizzily beyond of our
imaginations.

The theory and concept of 'island universe' had been developed by 18 century philosophers like Emanuel Swedenborg and Thomas Wright, but the later exponent with the actual term was Immanuel Kant. Footnote by trans.

★ 한글본 시 137쪽

The Solar System

The solar system

Is the ruin of the collapsed palace of a splendid nebula!

The eight planets,

Our moon

And sun

Are traces of the pillar, the rafter and the foundation, left

in ruins!

★ 한글본 시 138쪽

The Hole in the Universe

The big hole in the universe

Is the storehouse for piling up grudges of living creatures

Who were born in the universe,

But mournful about being ignorant of it.

Stars, the Moon and the Sun

The universe is in infinite darkness

But the stars,

The moon

And the sun

Are streetlights on its many corners to shine!

Its powerhouse is in the midst of the Creator's heart!

And the Moon and Sun are lamps for day and night, each

in the east and the west of Earth.

★ 한글본 시 139쪽

Earth´s Anchor

Is Earth a ship?
If so, the moon
Is anchor
Earth dropped in the sea of heaven.

The Factory the Sun Owns

Earth is one factory dealing with lives solely!

The supervisor of the whole work is the sun!

Earth is the biggest enterprise ever built by the sun!

Its product is "Happiness"!

Yet says the sun, 'Agony' is a "crude article"

Made by men against his will.

Earth and its Creatures

Earth

Is the pram wheeled by the sun;

The creatures

Are babies carried in it!

★ 한글본 시 140쪽

The Plants on Earth and Men

The plants on earth

Are

What the sun

Has germinated in the greenhouse called Earth

From the seeds chosen out of the 'cosmozon'(cosmic creatures)

and gathered.

Men are the gardeners to grow them.

★ 한글본 시 141쪽

The Sun's Offshoots

Earth is
One small seperate home
The sun set off for its creatures

So the sun
Would come every single morning in a sweat and hurry,
Pushing in to provide the creatures
Affectionately with heat, light, and clean air, to live on.

Fan of Sunbeams

The sun comes up every morning

With its fan of beams

And repel sleep from every creature's eyes

Just like driving the sparrows sitting on the crops away.

As the Sun Rises

As the sun rises,

The creatures open their eyelids

Like push opening a bush clover door of country home

calmly in the fog;

Baring their pupils like a full moon cleared off clouds;

Then would welcome the sun, cheering, arms up and wide

open.

Morning Dews on Leaves

The dews glistening

On the grass

And leaves of trees

That greet the sun

As it rises in the morning

Resemble the burning tears in the eyes

Of those in deep gratitude.

PART
II

Flowers by the Mountain
Road at Nightfall

To Greet the Morning

At tranquil dawn over city and country

The mountains, by their deep contemplation;

The roosters, by energetic cock-a-doodles;

The branches and twigs,

By waving their green handkerchiefs,

All greet the dawning soul of the morning.

The Moon and the Sun Playing Hide and Seek

The Sun is

An old widower in the sky

Living with his dear offsprings to care:

Moon, the daughter, and Earth, the son.

But the Sun, somehow, on some purpose

Put the siblings out in the air for racing drills day and night.

Stars Seated by the Moon

The little stars

By the moon,

Sit around the dressing stand,

Prinking up their faces, hair,

Front and rear

To greet the sun, their lover,

At the morn.

Above the Stars

Above the stars

Twinkling like the lanterns on the fishing boats

Amidst the night sky,

The spirit of night is serenely seated,

Pitching a net to catch all sounds from the souls on Earth.

★ 한글본 시 143쪽

The Flowers' Skirts

The heart of the sun

Is weaved up with rays of light in seven different colors:

violet, indigo, blue, green, yellow, orange, red.

Flowers on earth are dressed up

With skirts dyed thus.

Marigold(Gold Goblet Flower)

Yellow-trimmed

Purple petals;

The inner parts rolled in bill-shaped;

The marigold

Is a comely goblet for trees

To pour and drink nectar of pretty grass flower fragrance.

★ 한글본 시 144쪽

Flowers by the Mountain Road at Nightfall

Themselves primped

Charmingly

As the barmaid at tavern

To entice wayfarers,

The balloon flowers

In the valley

On the foothills

And elsewhere

Would hold the wind, bending down,

And wink quietly

At people.

★ 한글본 시 145쪽

Who Knows their Secret

On the seventh evening of the seventh month of the lunar
calendar

Altair and Vega, two stars, have rendezvous

In the high sky till so late at night, and who would know
their secret!

Ah, would anyone ever know it: being away from people's
eyes

Like a couple so intimate

Or secret agents from certain nation

They reunite once every year in the sky far and above

Who in the world would know their secret?

The Comet

The comet is
A nihilistic wanderer with cosmosism.

His long tail is
The pipe to sing the loneliness of wandering in space.

Yet the comet, if angry, would smash up the earth
With that long pipe.

The whole society of solar system wants to capture him,
For he's been under the heaviest surveillance, suspicious of
a rebellion conspiracy.

Moon under Water

The moon under water resembles

A ship at anchor in haven,

Loaded with souls of fish,

To sail for Milky Way.

Or, rather, it's a ship

That has carried wines of colors

Made of sweet dews,

Sent from the stellar world to the fish souls.

The Lunar Eclipse

The lunar eclipse is

The reunion Earth has

With his one and only sister,

Unforgettable,

Once in a long, long time in the air,

So glad and tearful; so adorable she is;

Thus carrying her on his back,

Hugging,

Then facing each other and rubbing on cheeks.

★ 한글본 시 146쪽

The Moon at Dawn

The moon just encountered with the early sun
Resembles a deserted wife living lonely,
Happened to see her husband going to work on time,
Would squint at him, then bang the door behind.

Roosters at Daybreak

The brood roosters

On perches,

Thinking they just got

Bundles of jewelry they held fast in dreams

Stolen by the black-hearted dawn,

Cock-a-doodle with the necks stretched forth.

Spring : Morceau de Poeme

Spring's skin,

Its smile,

And its mind can be touched:

It's the soft breeze brushing cheeks, tips of hair, yet startling!

★ 한글본 시 147쪽

Dew

Dew is milk,

So pure and fragrant,

Expressed down from the breasts of stars,

To feed leaves and flowers.

O Come, Swallows

Refugees coming from the sky!

Oh, poor immigrants air flown!

Ah, seeking shelter from winter wind;

To starve off hunger; each one in only suit;

Airborne like a flight of tiny planes swarming, your name is
Swallow

From the country of Aves!

O Swallows! We, the people of this nation, would not block
your landing.

We are going to give you eaves to stay,

The freedom to hunt abundant worms and insects to feed
you on,

And we'll let you have the calm breezes to warm your
bodies up.

Then we are all ears to your tales of wandering journey
around the world;

Hundreds of your reminiscent talks;

Your tweeting with accents and eloquence;

Well, gladly would we listen to all your checkered romances.

Oh, come, all Swallows,

To the paradise of spring in this country.

Butterfly just Got into a Flower

There's a yellow canna

With its bud barely open half way,

But a white and wily butterfly

Just flew into her.

The white butterfly

Got right into the yellow canna

Which's just like a house with none but a virgin,

Flying over then pushing in so slyly.

Multitude of Meteorological Observatories

We have whole lots of meteorological observatories

On the levees of rice paddy,

Even in the brooklets.

At each observatory

Is a meteorologist called frog,

Promoted and come from a tadpole.

Each frog has

This telescope in his big baggy eye

To check the conditions of the air and the sky.

When it's likely to rain,

They, with one accord, begin to croak.

And that's how they do weather forecast.

★ 한글본 시 148쪽

Madonna of Love

When Nature

Recreates the human lives,

Let its whole power of love

Be sent to the world of flowers.

So put all the human love

In the hands of flower;

Let them grow it forever.

Thus let the flowers

Be Madonna to teach the humans the way of love.

★ 한글본 시 149쪽

Spring

Spring's skirt is the east wind, its color green!

Spring's face is round and white as snow!

Spring's eyes are pink as a dove's!

Spring's heart is a fountain of love with honey hues!

Spring's occupation is manufacturing of lights; of songs!

Spring is the engineeress creating lovely lives!

She is the sun's youthful wife!

★ 한글본 시 150쪽

My Breath and Speech

I breathe in the air together with mountains, fields, seas and the earth.

I breathe along with hosts of stars, the sun and the moon, and the firmament.

I breathe together with the universe.

I breathe the air of the universe, along with even tiny ants and grass sprouts.

I breathe together with wild lions, tigers, nose to nose.

I share the sweet air with them, chewing it.

I breathe along with them in the expansion and contraction of the universe's lungs.

My blood of life, my heart, my wisdom and my soul are all endowed from the Mother Universe.

I laugh and weep along with the mind of the universe.

My speech, my songs are melodies that come out of the throat of the universe.

Though my speech conveys sound of universe,

It's dull with the most blunders.

★ 한글본 시 152쪽

Dahlia and Sunflower

The dahlia

At the foot of the fence wall

And the sunflower

Would brag about their heights

And stretch to be taller,

Standing on tiptoes daily, yet even before marriage

They stooped ; their flowers withered.

The Moon over the Brook

(at Sambang*)

The brook

Meanders through this vale and that vale;

Loaded with sad moans

Of trees and grass

That cannot walk, bound to the ground;

The moon also seems to have some sadness

Thus uncovering her chest over the flowing brook.

*

Sambang is supposed to be a rural town which has many cliffs, a gorge and
waterfalls. It's near Mount Masang, Anbyeon, Hamkyeong Namdo, (now in
North Korean part of Kangwondo).

PART
III

Symphony for Flowers

A Poem from Random Thoughts

The cricket is a vivid record of the autumnal sentiment,

Yet it is a clever son of that sentiment,

No, rather, its autumn's one tiny sprite.

Oh, cricket! I would cuddle that cute soul just like my child,

Stroke its head, and pat its rump lightly,

While paging through again in my dream today, the love
of Mother Nature.

Snow

The snow

Falls and flutters

Down from the sky,

But as to mountains and fields,

For thin trees and trembling grass

Which resemble a whole army

Of wounded soldiers bivouacked

In deep pains and fevers,

With cut faces,

Severed arms,

And crushed hands,

It applies medicine

With soft gauze bandages,

Even changing

At intervals.

And As to streams and brooks,

Where the wind,

Like a group of beasts of prey,

Would easily rage over,

Yet fish are used to be smiling,

Loaches dancing,

And water beetles whirling round,

It seals up waters

Standing

And running

Or covers

With thick glasses

That you cannot see through.

The Moonlight Adorable

Beside a brook

In the deep night

Of late autumn,

Holding my sleeve,

Would she ask, "Like to go to the sorghum field?

Or the mountain? Well, if not either,

Would we take ship

For an endless trip

Along the waterway revolving the earth,

Even up to the Milky Way?"

Though I shake off

No matter how hard,

One so persistent not to drop my sleeve tonight

Is my love, the Moonlight adorable.

A Letter

One day at dawn, a mailman

Came with a letter

Addressed, 'To: Humanity in Nature on Earth',

Throwing it on the ground.

On the other side of it is written: 'From: The Creator',

And in it reads: Dear Receivers: By the order of Time

Department, while the Summer and its whole family will be

taken back,

Mr. Autumn, beloved violinist of the Universe Orchestra

will be sent.

Therefore, in the Nature under the clear sky,

Fully enjoy variety of his masterpiece music played on his

strings: Song of Grass, Song of Leaves, Tune of Waves, etc.,

Crying in tears, feeling pathetic, and so on.

★ 한글본 시 151쪽

Autumn Nature's Ball

In autumn

The Mother Nature's great ball opens.

The water dances in brooks, rivers and seas,

Trees, in mountains,

And grass, in fields.

Yet they couple-dance with the wind, hugging each other.

The autumn wind is a male virgin, come to dance, dressed
in glorious tints of fall foliage,

To celebrate the victory for spring and summer of comely
laborers–water, grass and trees

On the stages by the brooks; on the rivers;

In fields, mountains and forests.

Stars

Stars are

The sky's descendants,

Born, and born beyond numbers

And grown cherished so precious

For several billion years.

They awake from sleep

Only at night,

Stick their heads

Out of mother's blue breasts,

Twinkle those eyes,

See down and talk about the wide world,

Purring every way: "Gonji, gonji"●

Or "Joem, joem"●● overnight.

●
Gonji, gonji : Korean baby language, meaning "Mark it, mark it" (with the pointer).
●●
Joem, joem : baby word to mean to close and open the fists.

Cosmos in Autumn Days

The cosmos

In the middle of the autumnal yard,

The floral society,

Sturdy with its long and slim waist straightened,

Looked so stately and solemn,

Having its green hair unkempt, yet standing aloft,

Resembles an inspiring philosopher or a revolutionist

In deep contemplation.

The Breeze

Trees

Hold up the breeze in their arms

To give it a swing as done to a baby.

Grass take the breeze's wrist,

For a hand wrestling: push and pull.

Waves,

Desiring to see its somersault,

Prepare a cushion-ripples-woven of smiles

From their eyes.

Radishes

Radishes,

Just like sticking a fist in the mouth of a savage beast,

Then glaring its eyes in a crouch,

They take strong root

In the ground.

The Flowers Soaked by Morning Dews

The flowers soaked with morning dews

Look like recently married women,

Exhausted by secret night pleasures,

That back of the hair got tangled,

And cheeks grown thin with sunken eyes.

The Sun Rising and Lowering

The sun rising in the dawn sky is like crawling out of and fleeing away from his fond girl's house, raided during sleep by a terrifying guy.

Or, it's like a big red diamond in one's fist being snatched up by people around.

Then sun lowering in the west is like being taken to the bed in a cellar, clasped by a bold and lewd woman who dares risking her life, or being carried away on a Samson's back, with the face covered up.

Also it reminds us a dad in a field being darkened, looking back tearfully at his little ones left behind, goes down the way, bowing his head.

Or, rather, he resembles the sorrow-stricken glitter of the eyes of a hero that dies young, so deplorable and reluctant to close eyes even at his end.

The Moon just out of Clouds

The pale-faced moon with sunken eyes

Just out of the clouds resembles one

Slipping out hurriedly, blushed, casting sidelong glances at
all around, adjusting herself,

After she did things secret: kisses, hugs and so on

With someone wandering she had met by the heavenly
roadside,

Behind the makeshift bedside screen formed with snatches
of clouds.

Moon on the River and the Sea

The moon

Reflected on the river

Or the sea

Reminds me a naked virgin with well-developed hips,

Playing in water.

Gang of Hoodlums in the Sky

In the night sky so calm,

Chunks of cloud, like naughty rogues or a gang of hoodlums,

Lurk, pitch camps of figured dark shades here and there

To catch and bother the comely-faced moon passing by.

★ 한글본 시 154쪽

Loose When Night Comes

The Sun

Puts the little baby stars

Like a pod of waterfowls in the sky

In its sleeves,

Then, when Night comes, loose them to flutter out.

Chicks out of Dream

The Night

Lets living creatures

Incubate 'eggs of sleep',

And hatch them into 'chicks of dream';

Waits till dawn;

Takes them all in birdcages, puts on his back, and is gone.

One Separate Thought

The sun,

Seen through the clouds thin and translucent,

Looks like a fearful eye of a famished tiger staring out of
water.

World of Pictures

Picture of clouds in the sky!

Picture of water, picture of grass, picture of trees on the earth;

—The whole world is a huge exhibition.

And the exhibitors are the sun and earth!

Men are the spectators!

Symphony for Flowers

Out of the shadow of rocks

Comely flowers call me.

Upto the tails of their eyes

And the sides of their mouths

They extend smiles, forming colorful heat haze,

And over the foreheads and cheeks

Wave their tiny palms of fragrance softly,

Gently, gently they call me.

Large butterflies, small butterflies, all come fly over here!

From under the shadows of rocks

Comely flowers call me.

By their cute smiles

And 'fragrant gestures'

They call me tenderly, tenderly.

Come on, let's go down!

How can we bear up not going beside the flowers?

Large butterflies, small butterflies, all come fly over here!

Now are we embraced by the beautiful flowers' smiles

And their fragrance,

Then are we going to drink our fills nectars, poured in the
cup of their stamina,

Drunk, intoxicated till we get shaken.

Shall we call for swallows in their black robes

To nimbly laud the greatness of the love of flowers;

Then we would request orioles to sing in their mellifluous
voices

The parables of love of flowers.

Would we call for the monkeys, genii of mimicking, to
play drums,

Also call for woodpeckers to hit the blocks made up with
living wood;

And make the green bees and red bees to buzz and hum
like a trumpet shell.

Let the magpies and and ravens recite the whole repertoires,

And have the male and female pheasants judge and announce in high voices the Merits and demerits, corrections.

For an extra entry, we'd invite the freshwater crabs for a wrestling match to Celebrate the occasion.

All Grass are to be "seated" in the shallow place,

But let trees stand where there are;

Put geese and cranes and storks high in midair;

Yet the butterflies big and small low,

Oh let them cover all over the sky in white or yellow,

Dividing into swarms to flutter here and there;

Dance and turn about in the air.

Let all ones fly, run, and crawl,

On the earth, grass and trees, in harmony,

Praise the love, souls and spirits of flowers with all-Nature symphony!

Flowers are sacred, despite they bloom on the branches of mere trees;

They love everything, and are loved by everyone.

Flowers are benefactors of love, and Nature's lovers.

O butterflies, swallows, canaries, monkeys, woodpeckers, bees green and red, Sparrows in mountain and field, male and female pheasants, freshwater crabs in The rice paddy and in the mountain brooks, geese and cranes!

Before the glory of the sun fades out,

Gather together be-side the flowers under the rocks,

Let us play with the symphony: rub-a-dub, tom-tom, te-dum-dum;

Sing and dance,

To laud the great love of flowers, the benefactors and lovers of nature.

Whoopie and hurray!

★ 한글본 시 156쪽

Fragrance of Flower

Flowers give forth fragrance, burning their own hearts.

Over the red flame of yearning love for the butterflies,

They burn the hearts and emit their perfumes.

★ 한글본 시 155쪽

Human Life

Man's body is a boat!

Man's soul is the boatman.

The man loads on the boat of body

Knowledge, gold, and hope,

Then, looking for the land of happiness,

Would it sail on across the ocean of torment,

But even in less than a mile it'd wreck on the rock called

"death."

★ 한글본 시 160쪽

Morning Glory

The morning glory

Opens its mouth

Smiling every morn

To kiss the rising sun

Of stately mien,

Then during the day and evening

Purses its lips-petals

Like a toothless grandma,

And keep them hidden

From others.

★ 한글본 시 161쪽

On the Poet Seokwoo Whang

Seokwoo Whang in 1920s
- From Jonghwa Park's Memoirs

Seokwoo Whang, Pioneer of Modern Korean Symbolic Poetry
- Shinkwon Cho, Professor Emeritus, Yonsei University

Seokwoo Whang in 1920s

The most significant poems in the first issue of Pehhuh can be said to be Whang's *The Sun sets, Blue Cat, Surrendering the Lover,* etc. In 1920s, the pioneer days of our free verses, the trend of poetry writing can be divided into two branches : symbolism and lyricism.

Four or five years later, as the literary professionalism arose along with the class leveling movement, some Whitman-like folk poems were produced, yet in its early stage, symbolical ones, which employed Western modern symbolism as well as our own symbolism, were prevailed.

Even though Joo Yohan's Fireworks is reckoned to be the first-ever Korean symbolical poem and I myself once viewed it in *Gaebeok* as an excellent symbolical verse, it has much of romantic lyricism. But, Whang's *the Sun Sets*(* see its text) in the initial *Pehhuh* was a symbolic poem of sagacity and keen intellect blended with dazzling sense of beauty.

The Sun Sets counts among his major works along with *Blue Cat*, and *Surrendering the Lover*, and it is like a splended silk sheet spreaded, weaved into from sounds, colors, hues, forms, and fragrances.

Whang was a man of talents, but not of virtues. It was a pity that he did not have fine pupils, hence rare people would sympathized with his poetry. But art is long, while life is short. His poetry will not perish.

Seokwoo Whang, joining in *Pehhuh* coterie, writes ten poems: *the Sun Sets, Blue Cat, the Sinking Sun, Surrendering the Lover, Palace of Lechery, Three Decisions, Poetic Tribute to the Deceased Mother, Ah, Miserable Visage, A Blood Poem, Encyclopedia,* but withdraws from *Pehhuh*, showing no work in the next issue which published on January 20, 1921.

The editor's comments of the issue clarified, "for several reasons Seokwoo Whang disaffiliated himself from *Pehhuh*". Besides the poor financial situation of *Pehhuh*, he was at odds with Yeom Sangsub and Namkung Byeok, the coterie novelists.

After quitting *Pehhuh*, Whang called in ones for his new junto to publish poems exclusively. Sooju Byeon Youngro, Gongcho Oh Sangsoon, Geunpo Sin Taeahk, Wooyoung Jeong Taesin, Noh Jayoung, Huiwol Park Younghee, me, Lee Hong, Lee Hoon, plus Park Indeok, a female member, all gathered at Bongwonsa, a newly open buddhist temple outside the West Gate. After discussions, they come to organize *Jangmichon*(i.e. Roses Town), Korea's first modern poetry coterie on May 24, 1921. Its publishing wing was located in

Park Younghee's house at 99 Cheongyeon-dong outside the West Gate. About that time Whang was studying plutonomy at Waseda University in Japan.

From Jonghwa Park's Memoirs

Seokwoo Whang, Pioneer of Modern Korean Symbolic Poetry

In 1920s when Seokwoo Whang were active, Korea was in a humiliating state of Japanese colonial rule. That Korean masses then were greatly influenced by Western liberalism as the modernism from the West floods. Especially Kim Uhg, Joo Yohan were heavily affected by french symbolism locked with fin-de-siecle mood, thus it would not be an exaggeration to say most of their writings around then were imitations, adaptations or re-creations of French symbolic works. Such move was reflexed in the whole literature that it generated the term "decadant romanticism". Later, in an effort of introspection, Kim Uhg, Joo Yohan, Kim Donghwan and Hong Sayong paid attention to folk songs and focused on writing folk verses, while Lee Sanghwa turned to tendency literature. Such an influx of western trends of lterature and publication of several coterie mags around this period let various approaches to and gropings of modern poetry possible. Korea's first-ever literary coterie magazine Changjo (i.e. Creation) published in 1919, was followed by *Pehhuh* in 1920, *Jangmichon* (i. e. Rose Garden) in 1921, *Baekjo* (i.e. Swan) in 1922, and *Joseon Moondan* (i.e. Korea Literary Circle) in 1924. Poetry about then still mostly inclined to nihilistic and decadant tendency that would deny any value. But the publication of *Jangmichon* led in a transition to romanticism.

Sangatab Seokwoo Whang(1895-1959), in his early days, was no exception to sing the closed fin-de-siècle circumstances. Most of his poems in *Pehhuh* tended so. But with the first issue of *Jangmichon* as a momentum, he converted to romanticism. In 1929, he brought out *Jayeonsong* (i.e. *Ode to Nature*), an anthology, which showed intensively the concrete results that he escaped from the chaos woven with imitations and indulgence to an independent world of creation out of self-awakening. Further, in his later years, Whang, totally deviated from the past decadence, gradually embodied isms and thoughts like devotion to Nature, the moving order of celestial bodies, generation principle of the universe, integration of omnia. Once he even inclined to tendency poetry to espouse socialistic ideas.

Whang was one who demonstrated sentience in Korean poetry for the first time, tried to sing celestial bodies sensorially. Also in the poems with nature sung, his sentience is revealed, making him a polestar. His writings include *Shihwa* (i.e. Poem Talk), *the Starting Point of Joseon Poetry Circles and Free Verses, Two Trends of Japanese Poetry World, Characteristic and Main Tide of Present Japanese Poetry Ideas.*

Not only Seokwoo Whang thusly left such a great legacy upon Korea's modern poetry, especially in 1920s, but also was he a remarkable patriot and independence activist. He, together with Kang Gideok, Bang Jeonghwan, and Oh Ilcheol, was active as one of Boseong College alumni, who involved in 3·1 Movement. And in 1940s, toward the end of Japanese colonial rule, he never yielded his fidelity to his own country, and held up indomitable spirit of resistance and identity as Korean even under severe oppression. Im Jonggook, a critic, in his 'Pro-Japanese Literature Criticism', listed 15 glorious anti-Japanese literary men: Yoon Dongjoo who died in prison in Japan; *Pehhuh's* Byeon Yongro, Oh Sangsoon and Whang Seokwoo; Lee Byeonggih and Lee Huiseung of Joseon Language Society; young poets like Jo Jihoon, Park Mogwol, Park Dujin, Park Namsoo, Lee hanjik; Nozak Hong Sayong who is said to be first to give up writing; Kim Youngnang, Lee Yooksa, Han Heukgoo and others. That suggests Sangatab being one of fervent nationalistic writer as well as an anti-Japanese poet.

Whang, though nihilistic to disavow any value earlier, had a major turn and then even attained a stage Joo Yohan and Kim Uhg could not follow after. Being metaphysical, his words are easy but have deep inner meaning. Unlike the other modernistic poets of 1930s, he would not run his words in technical arrays, but instead, he expressed in such a very artless manner and healthy imagery and poetic words thoughts of integrating universe through human purposes and experiences from the world of values.

Sangatab, almost like other romantist poets, regarded Mother Nature as a living organism breathing as the human. To him, Nature is like a human being who has a soul. Like human souls are immortal, Nature also has her own life, hiding mysteries within herself. Therefore Nature is not a simple creation by God but a voluntary agent which generates, changes and becomes extinct on its own. Nature is an object of senses and perception, not a thing itself to be explained scientifically and objectively, but is an organism that acts as a symbolic soul, and it has the world spirit within. It is unfair to judge Sangatab to be a mere decadent or nihilist from a glance of his early works.

He sure changed poetically with the publication of *Jang-michon*, and the closer to his end, the more he used sound and healthy imagery, harmonizing it into cosmic music. Thus, he created quite variant kind of poetry; hence more comprehensive and diverse revaluation of him is necessary.

Shinkwon Cho, Professor Emeritus, Yonsei University

편집자 일러두기

• 이 책 황석우 영역 시선은 고(故) 황석우 시인의 시 문집 중 1929년 발간된 《自然頌》과
  함께 기타 발표된 시를 중심으로 편저자가 중요도 높은 시를 채택해 구성하였습니다.
• 한글본은 원전에 근접한 초판본을 실었고, 띄어쓰기는 현대 표기법에 맞췄습니다.
• 이 책에는 영역 시 70여 편과 영역 시 중 일부를 채택해 한글본 30편으로 실었음을 밝
  힙니다.

황석우 영역 시선

웃음에
잠긴
우주

편저 박이도 | 영역 조신권

시간의숲

상아탑 황석우의 3남 황효영 씨를 만난 것은 지난 2014년 여름 미국 워싱턴 D.C.에서였다. 그는 어렸을 때부터 밖으로 떠돌던 부친의 부정(父情)을 별로 못 받고 자랐다고 했다. 또 모친께서 미국에 사는 따님 집으로 떠나는 연고로 청소년기부터 한동안 심정적으로 고아(孤兒)처럼 지냈다고 평생의 회한(悔恨)을 들려주었다.

황효영 씨도 미국 이민 40여 년을 살아오며 부친에 대한 혈육의 정을 술회하고, 시인으로서의 부친에 관한 이력을 자식과 손자들에게 전해 주어야겠다는 생각을 하고 있었다고 했다. 그 무렵 필자가 마침 황석우 시인의 작품을 소재로 쓴 짧은 에세이 한 편(서울·문학의 집 펴냄)을 전하고 장시간 황 시인에 관한 이야기를 나눌 수 있었다. 이런 이유로 '황석우 시선'을 번역판으로 출판하게 되었다.

고(故) 황석우(黃錫禹, 1895-1959년) 시인은 동인지 〈폐허(廢墟)〉(1920년)를 전후로 본격적인 활동 무대를 펼쳐갔다. 서울과 동경을 넘나들며 신문화 신문학에의 열정과 식민 치하의 이념적 고뇌를 안고 비평문과 자유시 창작에 몰두했다. 시집 《자연송》(1929년)에 수록된 것 외에도 많은 작품을 남겼다. 해방 이후에는 정치 활동과 교육계에서도 활발하게 활동하며 창작 활동도 이어갔다.

그의 시문학은 서구문학의 전수(傳受) 차원에서 〈폐허〉의 동인들과 자유시의 경작(耕作)에 집중했다. 그의 시적 발상법과 우주적 상상력은 특유의 개성의 미를 천착해 냈다. 특히 《자연송》에 수록된 상당수의 작품들에서 시적 대상이 된 자연 세계나 인물 등 사물에 대한 우주적 발상이나 상상력은 특유의 영역을 개척했다.

1959년 지병으로 사망 이후 황석우 시인에 대한 문학적 평가는 동시대에 함께 동인 활동을 했던 김억, 오상순, 김영랑 등에 비해 상대적으로 수면 아래로 사라졌었다.

최근 한국문단에서는 황석우 시인의 사적 위상과 문학작품에 대한 평가 작업이 활발하게 일어나고 있다. 정우택의 학위논문 〈황석우 연구〉를 비롯해 많은 연구 논문이나 에세이들이 발표되고 있다.

2016년 겨울

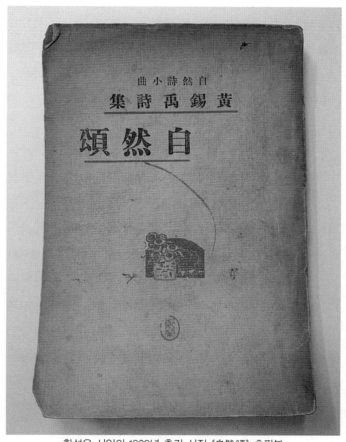
황석우 시인의 1929년 출간 시집 《自然頌》 초판본

1895년 경성부 천연동 16번지 출생

1911년 보성전문학교 입학, 3년 수료 후 보성전문학교 모표
　사건으로 퇴학

1914-15년경 도일

1916년 1월 16일 격월간지 〈근대사조〉 발간

1918년 미키로후(삼목로풍)가 주관한 미래사 동인으로 활동

1919년 2월 홍영우, 유지영, 이병도 등과 함께 동경 유학생 낙
　우회(樂友會)의 기관지 〈삼광(三光)〉 창간

1920년 4월 와세다대학(早稻田大) 전문부 정치경제학과 입학

1921년 5월 〈장미촌〉 창간(동인 변영로, 노자영, 박종화, 박영희, 정태
　신, 이훈, 오상순 등)

1921년 11월 25일 동경에서 원종린, 조용희, 정재달과 함께
　문화주의 운동 선전문을 배포하다 검거됨

1922년 7월 〈폐허(廢墟)〉 창간(창간 동인 김억, 남궁벽, 오상순, 이병도
　등과 함께 참여)

1922년 9월 제적. 〈삼광〉 3월호에 '고뇌(苦惱)의 려(旅)' 〈창조〉
　6호에 '눈으로 애인아 오너라', '소곡(小曲)' 등을 발표하며

여러 매체에서 활발히 작품 활동

1927년 2월 만주 장춘에서 만주이주조선농민보호연구회 부
　　회장으로 취임

1927년 10월 〈조선시단〉 창간

1945년 대동신문 주필 취임

1945년 12월 건국기금조성회 총무부에 참여

1946년 3월 전조선문필가협회 가입

1953년 4월 국민대학교 교무처장 취임

1955-58년 동아일보, 현대문학 등 각종 매체에 작품 활동 활
　　발히 함

1959년 4월 지병으로 영면

차례

 황글시   황석우 시선

● ──── 황석우 시인에 대하여

한글시

황석우 시선

落葉

落葉은
풀과
나무들의
그 産後의 몸 씨서 내리는 것

落葉은
풀과
나무들의 그 즐겁운 勞動의 自敍傳을
싸 우에 記錄하는 말, 그 굴근 글자

안개

안개는
한울이 쌜가벗고 옷 가러입느라고
재ㅅ빗 網紗로써
地球 우의
生物들의 눈을 가리워 놋는 것이랍니다

겨울을 尊敬하라

겨울을 尊敬하라
겨울은 偉大한 農夫이다
겨울은 어-ㄴ 쌍속에 봄을
봄의 아릿다운 生命을 심는 農夫!
흰눈은 곳 그 淨한 거름(肥料)!
또 한겨울 바람은 그 밧 가는 소의 씩ㅅ한 소리 외잇침!

반듸ㅅ불(童謠)

반듸ㅅ불은 잘도 날너단닌다
반듸ㅅ불은 얏흔 한울에서
반작반작
燈불을 켯다 껏다
풀밧 우로
시내ㅅ가로
나무가지 사희로
밤에 타는 才操 부리는 飛行機갓치
잘도 잘도 날너단닌다
아아 반듸ㅅ불의 날개 우에ㄴ
어대서 오신 누가 탓소
어대서 오신 누가 탓소

碧毛의 猫

어느 날 내 靈魂의
午睡場(낫잠터) 되는
沙漠의 우, 수풀 그늘로서
碧毛(파란털)의
고양이가, 내 고적한
마음을 바라다보면서
(이 애, 네의
왼갓 懊惱, 運命을
나의 熱泉(쓸는 샘) 갓흔
愛에 살적 삶아주마.
만일, 네 마음이
우리들의 世界의
太陽이 되기만 하면,
基督이 되기만 하면.)

夫婦配達夫

낫은男便, 밤은 안해!

둘은 永離別의 夫婦

그들의 生業은 配達夫

낫은 '勇猛서러운 精力―'을 配達하고

밤은 '平和로운 잠'을 配達한다

낫과 밤은 地球를 두便으로 난호와

낫은 太陽의 나라에서 勞動하고

밤은 별과 달의 나라에서 勞動한다

웃음에 잠긴 우주

어느 여름날의 이른 새벽이다

나는 잠 깨여 눈떴다

나의 머리맡에 와 앉은 꼬마 고양이도 눈 떠서 야옹한다.

고게 들어 창문을 열고 뜰아래를 보니

담 밑의 채송화들도 눈떠서 귀엽게 웃는다

하늘도 가슴프레 눈떠서 우슴을 흘리고

머ㅡㄴ 재아래의 아침 해도 눈떠서 빙그레 웃고 떠올라오
는 듯

왼 세계가 눈떠서 웃는 순간이다

우슴에 잠긴 우주다

夕陽은 꺼지다

젊은 新婚의 夫婦의 지적이는 房의
窓에 불그림자가 꺼지듯키 夕陽은 꺼지다,
夕陽은 꺼지다,
愛人아, 밤안으로 흠벅 우서다고,
나의 質素한 處女의 살갓흔 쌔굿한 마음을 펼(擴)쳐서
네 눈이 쌘시게 되도록, 너의게 뵈히마,
내 마음에는 지금 밧은
黃昏의
脈풀닌, 힘업는
哀痛한 接吻의 자욱이 잇슬 뿐일다.

愛人아, 밤안으로 흠벅 우서다고,
나의 이軟한 마음을 펴쳐
가을의 행그럽운 夕月을 싸듯키
네의 부닷기고, 孤寂한 魂을 싸주마.
愛人아, 밤안으로 흠벅 우서다고,
네의 우슴 안에 적은 幕을 치고

地球의 숫에서 기어오는 앙징한 '새벽'이
우리의 魂압헤 도라올 쌔신지
너와 니 야기하면서 쑬을 쌔듯키 자려 한다.

愛人아, 밤안으로 흠벅 우서다고,
네의 그 微笑는 처음사랑의
뜨거운 煌惚에 턱괴힌
小女의 살젹가(髮際)를 춤추어 지내는
봄저녁의 愛嬌 만흔 바람갓고
쏘 너의 그 微笑는
나의 울음 개힌 마음에 繡논적은 무지개(虹) 갓다

愛人아, 밤안으로 흠벅 우서다고,
나의 가쟝 새롭은 黃金의 叡知의 펜으로
네의 玲瓏한 우슴을 찍어
나의 눈(雪) 보덤 더 흰 마음 우에
黃昏의 키-쓰를 序言으로 하여

133

아ㅅ 그 哀痛한 키−쓰의 輪線 안에
너의 얼골(肖像)을
너의 긴−生涯를
丹紅으로, 藍색으로, 碧空色으로
네의 가쟝 즐기는 빗으로 그려주마.

愛人아, 밤안으로 흠벅 우서다고,
내 마음이 醉해 넘머지도록
너의 薔薇의 香氣갓고
處女의 살 香氣와 갓흔 속힘 잇는 웃슴을 켜(彈)려 한다
愛人아 우서라, 夕陽은 쩌지다.

愛人아, 밤안으로 흠벅 우서다고,
네 우슴이 내 마음을 덥는 한 아즈랑이(靄)일진댄
네 우슴이 내 마음의 압헤 드리우는 한 꼿발(화렴[花簾])일
진댄
나는 그 안에서 내 마음의 곱은 化粧을 하마,

134

네 우슴이 어느 나라에 길 쩌나는 한颱風일진댄, 구름일
진댄

　나는 내 魂을 그 우에 갑야웁게 태우마

　네 우슴이 내 生命의 傷處를 씻는 무슨 液일진대

　나는 네 우슴의 그 쓸는 坩堝에 쥐여들마,

　네 우슴이 어느 世界의 暗示, 그 生活의 한 曲目의 設明일
진댄

　나는 나의 귀의 굿은 못을 빼고 들으마,

　내 우슴이 나의게만 열어 뵈희는

　너의 悲哀의 秘密한 書帖일진댄

　나는 내 마음이 洪水의 속에 잠기도록 울어주마,

　愛人아 우서라, 夕陽은 쩌지다.

새벽

새벽 속에서 해가 떠오는 것이 아니다
햇빛이 나팔꽃과 같이 피어 벌려지는 때가 새벽이다
새벽은 햇빛의 만화병풍이 펼쳐지는 것이다
새벽은 해의 오랜지행기와같은 입김이 퍼져지는 때다
새벽은 머―ㄴ 해ㅅ발에 비치는 모든 생명의 빛이다
새벽은 햇빛의 첫행기에 취해가는 우주의 두 뺨 빛이다

小宇宙, 大宇宙

사람의 눈에 보히는 宇宙는

太陽界 둘네의 天體쑌임니다

그곳을 島嶼的 小宇宙라고 함니다

小宇宙 안에는 헤ㄹ크레스星雲의 別 宇宙 系統과 二億萬
의 몸 嚴壯한 별들이 한울 놉히 屛風과 갓치 둘너안저 잇고

그 밋으로 달과 太陽과 地球는 족으만 風扇 공과 갓치 귀
엽게 쩌돌아단님니다

이 宇宙 밧갓은 大宇宙, 그 안에 잇는 銀河의 저ㅅ족으로
저ㅅ족까지의

끗업는 無限에의

모든 '島嶼的 小宇宙'의 星雲, 쏘는 그들 星雲 속의 恒河
모래갓치 쌀니여 잇는

족으만 별들

太陽들

生物의 世界들은 그 種類와 數爻를 어즈러워 想像할 수도
업음니다

太陽系

太陽系는
華麗한 星雲의 殿閣의 험으러진 廢墟!
八 惑星과
달과
太陽은
그 廢墟 우에 남겨진 기둥, 석가래, 주초ㅅ돌들의 殘影!

별, 달, 太陽

宇宙는 끗업는 暗黑이온대

별과

달과

太陽은

그 곳곳의 洞里 목에 빗치는 街燈!

그 發電所는 造化翁의 心臟 속!

그리고 달과 太陽은 地球의 東西에 갈닌 晝夜燈이람니다

地球, 生物

地球는
太陽이 써는 乳母車
生物들은
그 우에 태인 太陽의 애기들!

地球 우의 植物, 人間들

地球 우의

植物들은

太陽이

'코스모존'(宇宙 生物)의 種子를 골나 모혀

地球라는 溫室 가운데 붓돗아 논 것이람니다

人間의 무리는 그 溫室의 植物을 갓구는 園丁!

아스츰 맛임

都會와 農村의 고요한 黎明 가운데서
山들은 깁흔 默念으로서
닭[鷄]들은 힘찬 노래로서
나무가지와 풀 가지들은
푸른 닙의 한케치푸를 흔들어
밝어 오는 아스츰의 魂을 마지합니다

별들의 우

밤한울 가운데
낙시배 燈불갓치 반작이는
별들의 우에는
밤의 精靈이 고요히 안저
地上의 만뢰(萬籟)의 魂을 그물질하고 잇담니다

금잔花

자지빗 바탕에
노란 주둥이의
쏫닙 옴으라진
금잔花는
나무들의
아릿다운 풀옷 香氣를 부어 마시는 그 고흔 盞이랍니다

저문 山길의 꽃

나그네 불너드리려는
山 주막의
색씨와 갓치
곱게 丹粧한
길경(桔梗) 꽃들은
골작이와
山기슬의
곳곳에서
바람을 붓잡고 허리 굽혀
사람들에게
은근히 눈짓한다

月蝕

月蝕은
地球가
단 하나의 니즐 수 업는
내 누이동생을
오래간만에 오래간만에 空中에서 相逢하여
눈물겹게 반갑고 귀여운 남어지에
등에 업어 보고
안어 보고
얼골 견우고 쌤 대여 보는 光景이람니다

봄 詩 斷章

봄의 살
봄의 우슴
봄의 마음은 만저 볼 수가 잇다
　그는 사람의 쌤에, 머리ㅅ털 긋헤 자즈러지게 스치는 보드
라운 微風!

數만흔 天文臺

논두렁과

개울에는

數업는 天文臺가 잇다

그 天文臺들에는

올챙이로붓허 榮轉헤 온

개구리라는 天文學者가 잇다

개구리들은

불숙 내밀은 큰 눈알을 望遠鏡으로 하여

눈부시는 듯히 찌긋이

한울 우의 氣像을 살펴보다가

비가 올 듯하면 一齊히 쌔굴쌔굴 울어 댄다

그것이 곳 개구리들의 비 온다는 ‘氣像 報告’란다

사랑의 聖母

自然이
人生을 다시 創造할 째에는
그 一切의 사랑의 힘은
쏫의 世界로 돌녀보내게 하여라
곳 人生의 모든 사랑은
쏫의 손에 맷겨
그를 永遠히 기르게 하여라
그리하여 쏫으로 하여곰
人生에게 사랑의 길을 가르키는 聖母가 되게 하여라

봄

봄의 치마는 東風, 그 빗은 草綠!

봄의 얼골은 동글고 눈갓치 희다

봄의 눈은 粉紅빗의 비둘기 눈!

봄의 마음은 숄빗의 사랑의 샘!

봄의 직업(職業)은 꼿 製造, 빗 製造, 노래 製造!

봄은 곳 아릿다운 생명(生命)을 맨드는 여류(女流) 기사(技師)!

봄은 太陽의 젊은 令夫人!

一枚의 書簡

어느 날 '새벽'의 遞夫가

地球國自然方

'人間殿'이라는 한 張의

便紙를 가지고 와서 地上에 내던진다

그 便紙 裏面에는 '造化翁 拜'라 하엿고

그 文面에는 日 '敬啓者 다름 안이라 TIME 府令에 依하여

여름과 그에게 딸닌 一切의 家族은 다려가고

宇宙 樂壇의 寵兒提琴家 가을 君을 보내니

한울 새로 물들인 맑은 大自然 속에서

가을 君의 바람 줄[風絃]을 타는

풀닙 曲調, 나무ㅅ닙 曲調, 물결 曲調 等의 여러 가지 名曲

을 울고 짜고 寒心 늣기여 마음것 享樂하라' 하엿더라

나의 호흡과 말

나는 산, 들, 바다와 함께, 대지와 함께 호흡한다.

나는 별의 무리, 해와 달과 함께, 창공과 함께 호흡한다.

나는 우주와 함께 호흡한다.

나는 우주의 대기 속에서 조그만 개미들과 풀싹들과도 함께 호흡한다.

나는 사나운 사자, 호랑이들과도 함께 코를 마조대고 호흡한다.

나는 그들과 우주의 달큼한 대기를 씹어 나눈다.

나는 그들과 함께, 우주의 허파의 신축(伸縮)과 함께 호흡한다.

나의 생명의 피, 나의 마음, 나의 지혜, 나의 혼은 우주의 모체(母體)에서 받은 것이다.

나는 우주의 마음과 함께 웃으며 운다.

우주는 나의 살의 신경이 통하는 전신상(全身像)이다.

나는 또한 우주와 함께 말한다.

나의 말, 나의 노래는 우주의 목 속에서 나오는 소리의 멜로디이다.

그러나 나의 말은 우주의 소리를 전하는 가장 오음(誤音)

많은 졸변(拙辯)이다.

空中의 不良輩

호젓한 밤한울 우에
不良輩 갓흔 선모습의 구름 뎅이가
군데군데 物形 그림자의 陳을 치고
길 가는 얼골 고흔 달을 붓잡어 굿찬케 시달닌다

꽃香氣

꽃은 그 마음을 태워서 香氣를 �뿜긴담니다
꽃은 꽃나비들을 思慕하는
빨간 사랑의 불꽃 우에 그 마음을 태워 香氣를 �뿜긴담니다

꼿 겻의 合奏樂

바위 그늘 밋헤서
아릿다운 꼿들이 나를 불은다
그 눈초리와
입가에 五彩의 아즈렁이를 일우는
우슴을 샐[膨]니고
그 니마 우로 쌤 뒤로
고사리 갓흔 적은
'馨氣의 손바닥' 살살히 내저면서
상양하게 상양하게 나를 불은다
큰 나비 작은 나비 모다 날너오너라
바위 그늘 밋헤서
아릿다운 꼿들이 나를 불은다
마음을 썰어 잡어 내리는
귀여운 우슴과
'馨氣의 손짓'으로
상양하게 상양하게 나를 불은다
가자, 가자 내려가자 우리들은

어이 저 솟들의 겻을 가지 안코 그대로 백일 것인가

큰 나비, 작은 나비 모다 날너오너라.

우리들은 저 아릿다운 솟들의 우슴에 안키고

馨氣에 안켜

그 솟솔의 盞에 부어 주는

花蜜을 마음것 켜[呷]고

醉해 醉해 醉해서 흐느러거리고

제비를 불너다간 法衣 입은 모습으로

쌔른 입으로 솟의 사랑의 偉大함을 말케 하며

쇠쏘리 불너다간 淸雅한 목청으로

솟의 사랑의 比喩를 노래케 하며

사람 흉내 잘 내는 잣내비를 불너다간 북[鼓] 치게 하고

啄木鳥 불너다간 사—ㄴ 나무의 木鐸 치게 하고

푸른 버—ㄹ 쌜간 버—ㄹ 불너다간 입 素螺 불게 하고

쌋치 쌈악이 불너다간 曲目 節次 외이게 하고

숫쑹 암쑹 불너다간 놉흔 소리로 長短 정정 멕이게 하고

番外로는 논 계[蟹] 산 계 불너다간 祝賀 씨름식히고

풀들은 얏흔 곳에 안치고

나무들은 그대로 세워 두고

기럭이와 鶴 두룸이는 놉흔 공중에

우리들의 큰 나비 작은 나비는 얏흔 공중에

희게 누르게 큰 한울 우를 덥허

제제로 난호여 이곳에서도 너울너울

저곳에서도 너울너울 춤추어 돌며

地球 우의

날으는 者 닷는 者 기는 者

풀도 나무도 한테 어울녀 全 自然 合奏樂으로써

꼿의 사랑―그 마음 그 魂을 讚美하자

꼿은 거룩하다 꼿은 微微한 植物의 가지 우에서 픠우나

그는 一切를 사랑하고 또는 一切에게 사랑함을 밧는다

꼿은 사랑의 恩人 그는 大自然의 愛人이다

오오! 나비, 제비, 쇠꼬리, 잣나비, 啄木鳥 푸른 버―ㄹ, 쌜
간 벌, 山 참새, 돌 참새, 수ㅅ꽁 암꽁 논 계, 山 계, 기럭이,
鶴 두룸이들아

太陽의 光明이 훗허저 쩌지기 前에
바위 밋의 꼿 겻헤 모혀
둥당둥당, 째째, 쌔쌔 管絃樂 잡혀
노래하며 춤추고
사랑의 恩人 大自然의 愛人 꼿의 偉大한 사랑을 얼사 조ㅅ
타 讚美하자.

人生

사람의 몸은 배(舟)!
사람의 魂은 그 배를 젓는 沙工!
사람은 그 몸의 배 우에
知識과 黃金과 希望의 짐을 실코
幸福의 陸地를 차저
苦痛의 大海를 쩌나가다가
一哩도 못 가서 死의 暗礁에 부딧쳐 沈沒해 버립니다

나팔쏫[牽牛花]

나팔쏫[牽牛花]은
아스츰이면
돗아오는 風采 조흔
太陽과 입 맛추느라고
우수며 입 벌겻다가
낫과 저녁이 되면
그 太陽과 입 맛춘 입술을
남에게 보히지 안으려고
니 째진 할미 모양으로
입술을 안으로 말어 옴으리고 잇담니다

황석우 시인에 대하여

박종화의 회고록-초기의 상징시(象徵詩)

－박종화(시인, 소설가, 비평가)

한국 초기 상징시의 기수 황석우

－조신권(연세대 명예교수)

박종화의 회고록—초기의 상징시(象徵詩)

〈폐허〉 창간호의 가장 무게 있는 창작시를 말한다면 황석우(黃錫禹)의 시 '석양은 꺼지다', '벽모(碧毛)의 묘(猫)', '애인의 인도(引渡)' 등이라 하겠다. 이때 1920년경 우리 자유시의 초창기에 있어서 창작을 시도한 시의 경향은 상징(象徵)과 서정(抒情) 두 갈래로 나눌 수 있다.

4, 5년 뒤에 계급 타파의 운동과 함께 프로문학적 경향이 대두되면서 휘트만식의 민중시가 제작되기도 했으나 초기에는 주로 상징시가 그 주류를 이루었다고 볼 수 있다.

우리의 상징주의는 물론 근대적 상징주의인 서구적 상징주의의 수법을 쓴 것이다.

주요한의 '불놀이'는 오늘날 문학사를 쓰는 이들이 한국 최초의 상징시라 했고 나 자신 역시 훌륭한 심볼리즘의 시였다고 〈개벽〉지에서 논평한 바 있지만, 주요한의 '불놀이'는 다분히 서정적 낭만이 흘러 있었다.

그러나 〈폐허〉 창간호에 실린 황석우의 '석양은 꺼지다'(본문 참조)는 백금 같은 예지와 현란한 미적 감각으로 교착된 재

기발랄한 상징시라 하겠다.

이 '석양은 꺼지다'라는 시는 '벽모의 묘', '애인의 인도'와 함께 그의 대표작으로서 마치 소리, 빛깔, 색채, 형상, 향기를 아름답게 교착시켜 짜놓은 한 폭 화사한 비단을 펼쳐놓은 듯하다.

그는 재(才)는 많으나 덕이 박했다. 좋은 제자를 두지 못한 탓으로 그의 시를 후세에서 알아주는 이가 드물게 된 것은 유감이라 하겠다. 그러나 시의 생명은 길다. 그의 시는 결코 소멸되지 않을 것이다.

시지(詩誌) 〈장미촌(薔薇村)〉

황석우는 〈폐허〉 창간호에 동인이 되어 '석양은 꺼지다', '벽모의 묘', '태양의 침몰', '애인의 인도', '음락(淫樂)의 궁(宮)', '세 결심', '망모(亡母)의 영전에 받드는 시', '참혹한 얼굴이여', '혈(血)의 시(詩)', '백과전서' 등 10편의 시를 발표한 후에 이듬해 1921년 1월 20일에 발간된 〈폐허〉 2호에서는 동인에서 탈

피했다.

〈폐허〉 2호 편집 여언에도 "여러 가지 사정으로 황석우 군과 〈폐허〉와는 관계를 끊게 되었다" 이같이 밝혀 놓았다. 〈폐허〉의 경영이 곤란한 중에 또다시 염상섭과 남궁벽과 의견이 맞지 않는 까닭이었다.

황석우는 〈폐허〉 동인에서 이탈이 된 후에 순수한 시만 발표할 동인을 모았다. 수주 변영로, 공초 오상순, 근포 신태악, 우영 정태신, 노자영, 희월 박영희 및 필자, 그리고 이홍, 이훈, 여류로는 박인덕을 참가시켜서 서대문 밖 새절 봉원사(奉元寺)에 모여 여러 차례 의논한 후에 21년 5월 24일에 한국 최초의 시지(詩誌)를 창간했다. 이것이 곧 〈장미촌(薔薇村)〉이다. 이때 장미촌사(社)는 서대문 밖 천연동(天然洞) 99번지 박영희 집에 두었다.

황석우는 일본 와세다대학 정치경제과에 재학 중이었다.

박종화(朴鍾和, 시인, 소설가, 비평가)

한국 초기 상징시의 기수 황석우

황석우 시인이 활약한 1920년대에 있어서, 한국은 일제의 식민지라는 굴욕적인 상태에 놓여 있었다. 당시의 한국 민중들은 서구의 자유주의 사조에 영향을 크게 받았다. 특히 김억, 주요한은 프랑스 상징주의의 영향을 크게 받았는데 이 시기에 창작된 작품들 대부분이 세기말적 시대 상황과 맞물려 프랑스 후기 상징주의 작품을 모방하거나 개작 재창작하였다 해도 과언이 아니다. 이런 기류가 문학 전반에 반영되어 퇴폐적 낭만주의라는 용어를 낳게 되었다. 그 이후 반성의 일환으로 김억, 주요한, 김동환, 홍사용 등은 민요에 주목하여 민요시 창작에 힘쓰게 되었으며 이상화 등은 경향문학으로 전향하게 되었다.

이 시기에는 이와 같이 서구 문예사조의 유입과 여러 동인지의 간행을 통하여 현대시의 다양한 모색이 이루어졌다. 1919년에 창간된 최초의 문예 동인지 〈창조〉에 이어, 1920년에는 〈폐허〉, 1921년에는 〈장미촌〉, 1922년에는 〈백조〉, 1924년에는 〈조선문단〉 등이 나오게 되었다. 이 시기의 시들은 대체

로 일체의 가치를 부정하는 허무주의적이고 퇴폐적인 경향을
띠고 있다. 그러나 〈장미촌〉 창간은 낭만적 경향으로 기울게
한다.

상아탑 황석우(1895~1959)는 예외 없이 초기에는 폐쇄적이
고 세기말적인 정황을 노래하였다. 〈폐허〉지에 발표되었던 시
들은 대부분 그러한 경향을 띠고 있다. 그러나 〈장미촌〉 창
간을 전후로 하여 시적 전환을 시도해 낭만적 경향으로 기울
어지게 된다. 상아탑 황석우는 1929년에 《자연송(自然頌)》이라
는 시집을 간행함으로써 그동안 모방과 파탄으로 얼룩진 혼
돈에서 벗어나 자아 각성을 독자적인 작품 세계로 구체화한
성과를 집약해 보여주게 된다. 더욱 말년에 이르러서는 시대
적 퇴폐성에서 벗어나 점차 천체의 운행 질서와 만유의 생성
원리 및 만상의 일체화 곧 자연애의 귀의와 같은 사상을 형
상화하였고, 한때는 사회주의적인 사상을 표방하는 경향시
(傾向詩)로 기울어지기도 했었다.

황석우는 한국 시가에서 감각성을 최초로 보여준 시인인데, 천체에 대한 노래를 감각적으로 구사하려 하였다. 한편 자연을 노래한 시에서도 감각성을 엿볼 수 있어, 주목을 끌었다. 시집으로는 《자연송(自然頌, 1929)》이 있고, 시론으로는 《시화(詩話)》 외에 《조선 시단의 발족점과 자유시》, 《일본 시단의 2대 경향》, 《현 일본 시상계의 특질과 그 주조》 등이 있다.

황석우는 한국의 1920년대 현대 시사에 큰 공적을 남겼을 뿐 아니라, 독립운동가와 민족혼을 지킨 지사로도 유명하다. 그는 강기덕(康基德), 방정환(方定煥), 오일철(吳一澈) 등 3·1운동에 적극 가담했던 보전(普專) 인맥의 일원으로 활약하였고, 일제 말기인 40년대에는 강한 탄압 속에서도 조금도 지조를 굽히지 않고 민족정신을 끝까지 지킨 철저한 저항 정신의 체현자였다. 비평가 임종국은 《친일문학론》에서 영광된 반일 작가로서 옥사한 윤동주, 〈폐허〉파의 변영로, 오상순, 황석우, 조선어학회 관련 이병기, 이희승, 젊은 시인으로 조지훈, 박목월, 박두진, 박남수(朴南秀), 이한직(李漢稷), 제일 먼저 절필했다는 노작(露雀) 홍사용을 비롯해서 김영랑, 이육사, 한흑구(韓黑鷗) 등 총 15명을 들고 있다. 이로 미루어 볼 때 상아탑 황석우는 한국 근대의 반일 시인으로도 기억되는 민족주의적인 작가라 할 수 있다.

황석우는 한국 근대 상징주의 시운동의 기수로서 초기 시에서는 대체적으로 일체의 가치를 부정하는 허무주의적인 경향의 시만을 쓴 시인이다. 그러나 말년에는 시적인 전환을 통하여 주요한이나 김억이 따를 수 없는 경지에까지 이르러 말은 쉬우면서도 속뜻이 깊은 형이상시적인 시를 썼다. 그는 1930년대 활동한 다른 모더니즘 시인들처럼 언어의 기법적인 배열 위주로 치닫지 않고, 인간적인 목적과 가치 세계의 경험을 통한 우주의 일체화 사상을 아주 소박하면서도 건강한 이미지와 언어로 표현해 주었다.

상아탑은 다른 낭만주의 시인들과 거의 같게 자연을 사람처럼 숨 쉬는 유기체와 같은 것으로 파악했다. 자연이 영혼을 가진 인간의 존재와 같으며, 인간의 영혼이 영원불멸하듯 자연 역시 스스로의 생명력을 가지고 그 내면에 신비함을 감추고 있다고 생각했다. 따라서 자연은 단순히 신의 피조물이 아니며, 그 자체로 생성, 변화, 소멸하는 자발적인 실체이다. 자연은 감각과 지각의 대상물이며 과학적, 객관적으로 해명될 수 있는 사물 자체가 아니라 영혼의 상징체로 활동하는 유기체이며, 세계의 정신이 내재한다고 생각했다. 상아탑의 초기 시만 보고 그를 퇴폐주의자 또는 허무주의자로 치부하는 것은 옳지 않다.

그는 〈장미〉의 출간을 계기로 시적인 전환을 했고 말기로 갈수록 아주 건전하고 건강한 이미지를 사용해서 우주의 일체화 또는 천체 음악으로 표상하였다. 황석우는 이와 같이 매우 다양한 성향의 시를 썼으므로 그에 대한 연구도 좀 더 총체적이고 다양히 평가하여야 함이 마땅하다.

조신권(趙神權, 연세대 명예교수)

황석우 시인의 《자연송》 초판본
—

Seokwoo Whang's *Ode to Nature*(first edition)

황석우 시인(1895-1959)
지인이 그린 황석우 시인의 모습

—

A portrait of the poet (1895-1959)
painted by an acquaintance

황석우 시인의 부인 윤덕상
아래 친필 글은 황석우 시인의
아들이 보관한 모친 윤덕상이 쓴 글
(자신에 대하여 기록한 내용이 인상적이다.)

—

Yoon, Deoksang, the poet's wife (with
an impressive note on herself in her own
handwriting)

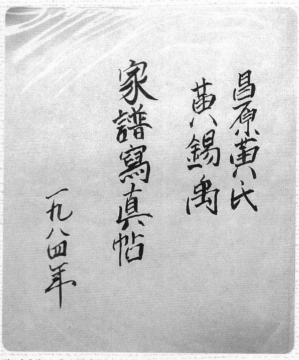

昌原黃氏
黃錫禹

家譜寫眞帖

一九八四年

황 시인의 부인 윤덕상이 1984년에 친필로 기록한 가보사진첩
—
A family treasure photo album containing Deoksang's notes written
in 1984.

미국 워싱턴 D.C.에 사는 황석우 시인의 3남 황효영 씨 부부
Hyoyoung (the poet's third son) and his wife who live in Washington, D.C.

그는 미국생활 40여 년 이민자로서의 삶 속에서 부친 황석우 시인을 회고하는
글과 시, 시인에 관한 이력을 교포 후세대 자녀손들에게 전해 주고 싶은 바람을
이 영역 시선집에 담고 있다. 세대를 아우르며 세계화 속의 젊은 세대에게도
그 시대 상징시의 의미를 전하고자 한다.
—

Hyoyoung, an immigrant for more than forty years, has waited so long for
an anthology of his father's poetry translated into English, such as this, to be
published. That is, his long-cherished desire to pass on to the next generation
the main works and a glance at the life of the late one who was an exponent
of Korean decadentism and early modern symbolism, can be said as realized
partly in this little book.

시간의숲은 당신의 시간 속에 자라는 지혜의 나무입니다.

Selected Poems of Seokwoo Whang – English Translation
황석우 영역 시선

Universe Full of Smile
웃음에 잠긴 우주

—

초판 1쇄 발행 2017년 2월 17일

—

편 저 박이도
영 역 조신권
펴낸이 임영주
펴낸곳 시간의숲
주소 경기도 성남시 분당구 서현로 216, 707호(서현동, 오벨리스크)
전화 070-4141-8267
팩스 070-4215-0111
전자우편 book-forest@naver.com
홈페이지 sigansoop.com
등록 제2016-000001호(2016년 1월 4일)

—

디자인 WI

—

ISBN 979-11-957491-3-3 03810
정가 10,000원

이 도서의 국립중앙도서관 출판예정도서목록(CIP)은 서지정보유통지원시스템 홈페이지
(http://seoji.nl.go.kr)와 국가자료공동목록시스템(http://www.nl.go.kr/kolisnet)에서
이용하실 수 있습니다.(CIP제어번호: CIP2017000333)